Michael Broad lives in Surrey on Planet Earth, where he writes and illustrates books for children of all ages, including the Jake Cake series, which was shortlisted for the Waterstone's Prize. Michael loves dogs, daydreaming and anything to do with astronomy.

www.michaelbroad.co.uk

Other books by Michael Broad

Spacemutts: Fluffy Assassins from Mars!

Spacemutts: Attack of the Ninja Kittens!

Spacemutts: The Hairball of Horror!

MICHAEL BROAD

SPACE MUTTS
THE SAUSAGE DOG OF DOOM!

MACMILLAN CHILDREN'S BOOKS

First published 2012 by Macmillan Children's Books
a division of Macmillan Publishers Limited
20 New Wharf Road, London N1 9RR
Basingstoke and Oxford
Associated companies throughout the world
www.panmacmillan.com

ISBN 978-0-330-51142-1

1 3 5 7 9 8 6 4 2

A CIP catalogue record for this book is available from
the British Library.

Printed and bound by CPI Group (UK) Ltd, Croydon CR0 4YY

For Bella

(a lovely Labrador)

The Alien Invasion

Have you ever looked up at the stars and wondered if aliens really exist? Well, they do! Lots of them! All across the galaxy bright green eyes are looking right back at us, studying our world as they prepare to invade it.

Some aliens already walk among us, but they don't have slimy skin or wiggly tentacles. They're cute and fluffy, eat fish and chase mice, and if they're not already living in your home, you've probably seen them in your garden.

That's right – all cats are aliens from outer space! Tiddles from next door is in charge of weapons. Pickle from the post office relays intergalactic orders. And the big ginger tom who lets you tickle his belly on your way to school is an expert in explosives.

It's true that some cats are harmless and happy just being our pets, but if you watch the others closely you'll see they're up to something. Most of them are spies, plotting in secret and preparing for the invasion. Cats have ruled the rest of the galaxy for thousands of years, conquering every habitable world, and now their sights are set on Earth to complete their evil empire.

The feline forces have tried to invade

our planet many times before, which is how so many cats got stranded here. But they were always doomed to fail because Earth is home to the best alien defence force in the universe . . .

THE SPACEMUTTS

When night falls on the Pooch Pound

dogs' home, these courageous canines

board their spaceship and patrol the

galaxy. Man's best friend defending

the Earth against cosmic kitty cats.

THE DOGS

ROCKET Fearless leader
of the Spacemutts

POPPY Plucky pilot of the
spaceship *Dogstar*

BUTCH Inventor, dribbler
and all-round genius

OSCAR New recruit
(a yappy mini
dachshund)

THE CATS

LADY FLUFFKINS Evil empress of the entire galaxy (well, almost)

BALDY Cowardly minion of Lady Fluffkins

THE FELINE FORCES Every breed of cat across the galaxy!

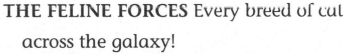

Contents

Yappy to See You

Running towards the exit with their hands pressed over their ears, the visitors to the Pooch Pound couldn't leave fast enough. They passed Poppy, who was spinning in circles and snapping at her

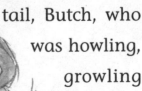

tail, Butch, who was howling, growling

and frothing at the mouth, and Rocket, who was barking at the top of his lungs. But as the family fled the kennels and the warden closed the door behind them, only one dog could still be heard above the din.

 barked the mini dachshund in the fourth kennel as he raced around on his tiny legs. Oscar was only small, but his voice was so loud and high-pitched that it bounced off

the bare brick walls and rattled the metal bars.

'That's the fifth family he's seen off today!' yelled Poppy, ceasing her tail-chasing and folding her ears down to block out some of the noise. 'He'll never be rehomed if he keeps this up!'

'He's hardly stopped yapping since he arrived this morning!' yelled Butch, wiping the drool from his mouth and pulling his blanket over his head to muffle the sound. 'If he carries on, that sausage dog will put me off sausages for life!'

'Really?' gasped Poppy, knowing how much the bulldog loved food, and sausages in particular.

'No, probably not,' Butch admitted.

As the racket continued, the two dogs looked helplessly at Rocket, knowing he was the only one who could silence the dachshund. The big brown mutt nodded for his kennel mates to cover their ears, then he leaned forward and took a long, deep breath.

Rocket boomed.

The volume of the blast snapped the sausage dog out of his yapping frenzy, but he was only silent for a few seconds before he turned towards the other dogs and started wagging his tail enthusiastically.

'That last family will be taking me home for sure!' yapped Oscar. 'Did you see how quickly they rushed out of here to tell the warden they want me?'

'We saw them running,' Poppy said, frowning.

'They were definitely in a hurry,' Butch added uncertainly.

'I don't think they'll be coming back again, Oscar,' Rocket added kindly. 'We told you when you arrived that the people who come to the Pooch Pound usually go for the quieter dogs.'

But I get so excited when they come in!

gasped Oscar, yapping three times at the thought of it. 'And I'm quite small and low down, so they probably wouldn't see me if I didn't get their attention.'

Sometimes it's smart to be silent,

said Rocket.

'You three always make a racket when the families arrive,' said Oscar, eyeing them suspiciously. 'Maybe you don't want them to notice me so they'll pick one of you instead.'

'We wouldn't do that,' said Rocket.

'We can't let anyone take us home,' said Poppy. 'Not yet, anyway.'

'That's why we go bonkers when the visitors come,' said Butch.

'Why should I believe you?' said Oscar, remembering his last home with sadness. 'All dogs want a family who will love them and look after them even if they yap when they're left alone all day. I don't see what makes you three so different.'

Maybe we should show him,

said Rocket.

Show me what?

yapped Oscar.

SPACEMUTTS

yapped Oscar, and because he wasn't getting any answers he continued to yap, yap, yap in the background while the three dogs decided on the best course of action.

'It's the only way he'll trust us,' explained Rocket, tilting his head at the sound of the warden's squeaky new boots as he locked up the Pooch Pound for the

night. 'And if he makes a racket when we leave, someone might investigate and find us three missing.'

Poppy and Butch nodded in agreement and began clearing away chew toys and bowls, before bunching up their blankets and taking a seat in the centre of their kennels.

'YAP?' yapped the dachshund, wondering what was going on.

'Move into the middle of your kennel, Oscar,' said Rocket, turning away to swipe his collar, which made its spikes light up around his neck. 'This is Rocket

calling the *Dogstar*,' he said. 'Come in, *Dogstar*.'

'Hello, Captain,' said the female voice of WOOF, the spaceship's onboard computer. 'The *Dogstar* is orbiting Earth above your location and all systems are prepped for boarding. How many dogs need teleporting this evening?'

'Three and a half,' Rocket said with a smile, watching the mini dachshund dashing around on short little legs, clearing away toys and bowls as Poppy and Butch had done.

'A half?' said WOOF. 'That does

not compute, Captain.'

'Make that four,' said Rocket, remembering that WOOF was a computer and didn't really understand his jokes. 'Over and out,' he added, and moved into position.

The three Spacemutts watched as Oscar bunched up his blanket and trotted to the middle of his kennel, yapping so many questions that he didn't even notice when the overhead dome-lights flickered on and off.

'In space, no one can hear you yap!' smiled Rocket as four shafts of light shot

down from the
ceiling.

'No one except
us,' Poppy and Butch
sighed together.

The four dogs suddenly sparkled
and shimmered in the brilliant light
beams and then disappeared one by
one. Rocket was the first to go, quickly
followed by Poppy and Butch. Oscar was
the last to leave, but before he vanished
the sausage dog stopped yapping long
enough to utter a very loud 'HUH?'

Far across the solar system, the clockwork *Mouseship* hovered in close orbit on the dark side of Jupiter where it could not be detected from Earth. At the observation deck, Lady Fluffkins watched as a giant hose pumped gas from the planet into a vast white balloon that wobbled in the sky.

'It's working, Majesty!' gasped Baldy. 'It's beginning to take shape!'

'Of course it is, you cat-shaped worm!' hissed the empress, green eyes

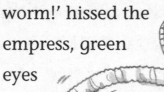

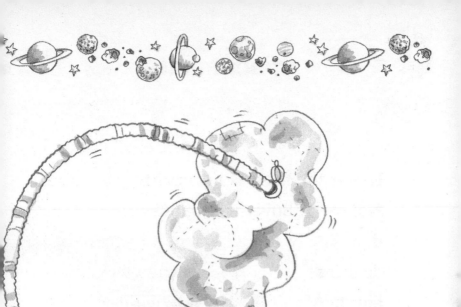

glaring at her mammoth masterpiece. 'This has been years in the making. Nothing can possibly go wrong.'

The hairless servant's wide eyes widened even further as the colossal blob continued to swell, blotting out the stars and filling the inky night with its dazzling whiteness.

'It is the most wonderful thing I have ever seen!' Baldy whispered.

The most wonderful?

growled the empress, pulling on sunglasses to protect her eyes from the sudden glare. 'Would you like to take a moment to think about that?'

The meek minion gasped when he realized what he'd said.

'Er, except for you, M-M-Mistress!' he stammered. 'Nothing in the whole universe is as wonderful as you. You are the most wondrous of wonders!'

'Yes, I am,' spat the empress, flicking the underling away with a swift swish of her tail before kicking the levers to shut off the hose. 'And my cunning craft is finally complete!'

'Does that m-m-mean . . .' said Baldy, looking slightly more petrified than usual.

'Yes,' said the empress. 'It is time to load my deadly weapons!'

'Are they *really* as deadly as they say?' whispered Baldy.

'Deadlier,' grinned the empress, drumming her claws on a monitor that was showing a live feed of Earth. 'They will devastate that little blue planet and complete my empire by morning, and there's nothing those fleabag dogs can do to stop them.'

Jumping to Jupiter

As the four teleport beams sparkling on the transportation deck of the orbiting *Dogstar* faded away, four dogs were standing in their place. The three regular Spacemutts quickly bounded to their stations, leaving Oscar gazing about the spaceship with wide eyes and an open mouth that was uncharacteristically silent.

The stunned sausage dog saw Poppy in the cockpit, her expert paws moving over the controls as she switched the *Dogstar* from autopilot to manual. He saw Rocket standing upright at the central hub, scanning data from local satellites and deep-space telescopes. Then he looked around to find Butch snuffling through his toolbox and examining the engines at the rear of the massive metal craft.

The dazed dachshund shook his head, making his floppy ears flap, then he leaped from the deck and made up for lost time by yapping all of his questions

at once, dashing from station to station like a wild thing.

'Where are we? What's that big blue ball? Is it planet Earth? Are we in space? How did we get here? What does that do?' he yapped, on and on, getting louder and faster, until he was racing in circles and yap, yap, yapping.

The sound bounced around *Dogstar*'s metal belly and was so loud that Poppy  pulled on her headphones and Butch shot under the white sheet that  covered his latest invention. Rocket was left to deal with the noisy new recruit, so he pressed the intercom button on the central hub and leaned forward.

'OSCAAAAR!' he yelled into the microphone.

The booming speakers made the spaceship rattle, shaking the

sausage dog into seated silence. Oscar then sat panting in front of Rocket while the captain explained all about the Spacemutts and their role in fending off Lady Fluffkins and her feline forces.

'Cats rule the whole galaxy?' yapped Oscar.

'All except for planet Earth,' said Poppy, pulling off her headphones.

'That's why we behave badly at the Pooch Pound,' said Butch, waddling out from under the sheet. 'We can't go to new homes until we've captured Lady Fluffkins.'

'I'm sorry I doubted you all,' said Oscar, and began a swift sniffing tour of the spaceship, yapping his way through the millions of questions he still had about the Spacemutts. Poppy and Butch took turns to answer him from their stations, while Rocket returned to the central hub to finish analysing the *Dogstar*'s security data. All of the information seemed to be in order, until he noticed that one of the files was missing.

'WOOF,' said Rocket, calling out to the ship's computer.

'Yes, Captain?' replied the female voice.

WOOF was short for World Orbiting Observation Facility, which among other things involved gathering data from far across the galaxy and feeding it through the central hub for the captain's sharp-eyed analysis.

'We seem to be missing one of the spy-ball satellites,' said Rocket, double-checking the screen and keying in the location code. 'Can you show me which one it is so that a replacement can be dispatched?'

'Right away, Captain,' said WOOF.

The monitor over the hub immediately

displayed an electronic map of the galaxy and a scrolling list of numbered coordinates. One of them began flashing red and the map zoomed in on its location.

'Jupiter?' said Rocket, as an image of the giant gas planet filled the screen.

'Affirmative,' said WOOF. 'The signal was lost one hour ago.'

'That's unusual,' said Poppy, swinging round in the cockpit seat. 'Meteorites often take out satellites in deep space, but we've never lost one this close to home before.'

'The spy-balls are very small,' said Butch, who had made them all himself using tennis balls and tinfoil. 'Jupiter's gravity field could easily have sucked one in. The planet is like a massive magnet to anything that comes too close.'

'Can we go and fetch it?' yapped

Oscar, feeling left out.

'I think we'll have to,' said Rocket, rolling out a star map to calculate the distance. 'We can't have a blind spot in our own solar system. Jupiter is only twenty minutes away from Earth travelling at the speed of light, which is too close for comfort.'

Firing up the light-speed engines now, Captain,

said Butch, pulling levers and adjusting

pressure valves until the back of the ship groaned and hissed with the sudden surge of power.

I've plotted a course for Jupiter,

said Poppy, programming the instruments on the pilot's control panel before resting her paws on the acceleration levers.

'Countdown whenever you're ready, Butch,' said Rocket, bounding over to the pilot station. The captain saw Oscar sitting in the middle of the floor yapping unhappily to himself and called him up to the front of the ship. 'There's a better view from here, little one,' he said.

The dachshund hurried forward wagging his tail excitedly and Rocket lifted him up on to the control panel. As Oscar stared through the observation window howling with excitement Butch began the countdown.

Light speed in five, four, three, two, one!

he barked.

SPACEMUTTS

On the count of one, Poppy pushed down on the levers and the *Dogstar* shot though the starry night like a blazing comet, passing Earth's moon in the blink of an eye, swerving around Mars and weaving through the rocky asteroid belt on its way to Jupiter. As they travelled at the speed of light, only one voice could be heard asking the same question over and over again.

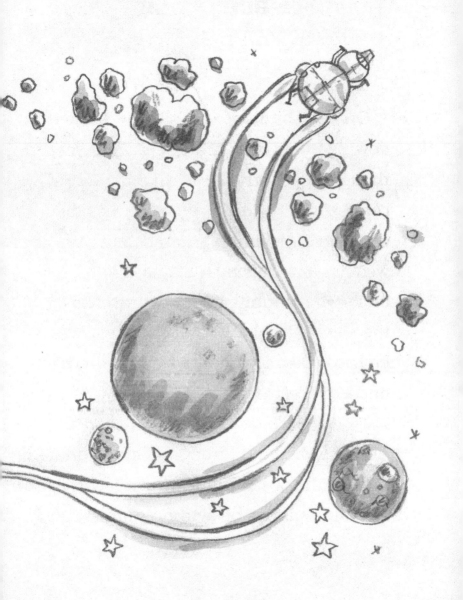

yapped Oscar, unable to contain his
excitement. He only stopped asking when
the great orange ball appeared in the
distance, growing larger and larger until
it filled the observation window with its
churning surface of swirling storms.

'WOW!' gasped the new recruit as they entered the gas giant's orbit.

The mini dachshund was used to feeling small next to bigger dogs and humans, but compared to the super-massive planet Oscar felt like a tiny speck of dust.

'Impressive, huh?' said Rocket, returning to the central hub.

'Jupiter is the biggest planet in our solar system,' said Butch, shutting down the light-speed engines and stabilizing the ship. 'It's bigger than all the other planets put together!'

'And it has lots of little moons!' said Poppy, hopping down from the cockpit to stretch her legs. 'You might be able to spot one yourself if you look very closely.'

'There's one!' yapped Oscar, pressing his nose against the glass as he scanned the starry sky. 'Though it's a bit of a funny shape. More of a lumpy blob than a proper round moon.'

The Spacemutts all stopped what they were doing and raced to the front of the ship. There they leaped up to the control panel in time to see a pale, hazy object creeping over the north pole of Jupiter.

'It's leaving the planet's gravity field,' gasped Poppy, as the strange shape continued to rise instead of following a circular lunar orbit. 'Maybe it's a runaway moon?'

'One that bounces off its own magnetic field?' Butch frowned. 'With the speed that thing is travelling it's more likely to be a rocket, but Jupiter has no solid ground to launch from.'

'It's not a moon or a rocket,' said the captain.

'How can you be sure?' asked Poppy and Butch.

'Because it seems to be changing course!' said Rocket.

The Spacemutts' mouths dropped open as the white blob slowly halted its upward trajectory, paused in mid-air and then took off in another direction.

'Where's it going?' yapped Oscar, jumping up and down to get a good view through the observation window as Rocket, Poppy and Butch all leaned forward at the same time. 'Can we follow it?'

'No need!' said Rocket. 'It's heading straight for us!'

As well as changing course, the colossal object was picking up speed, growing larger and more distinct as it shot towards the *Dogstar*. And the closer it came, the more vivid and unbelievable it seemed.

'It can't be,' said Poppy, as the true size and shape were revealed.

'What is it?' pleaded Oscar, jumping higher. 'Is it a bird or a plane?'

'No,' drooled Butch. 'It's a giant bone!'

'Correction,' growled Rocket, as the massive morsel soared overhead, dwarfing the *Dogstar* and casting a vast shadow over it. 'It's an alien airship *shaped* like a bone. And it's not heading for us – it seems to be right on course for planet Earth!'

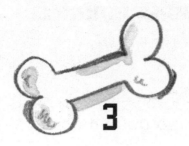

3

The Howling

As the bone-shaped airship soared
overhead, Butch ran to the cannon at
the back of the *Dogstar* and pulled the
lever to dispatch a replacement spy-ball
into Jupiter's orbit. Then Poppy swiftly
turned the ship round and took off after
the curious craft.

'It has to be Lady Fluffkins,' said

Rocket, pacing up and down. 'She must have disabled the satellite remotely and used the blind-spot to make a wormhole jump straight into our solar system.'

'Does she really think we'll see a big juicy bone and just let it pass?' said Butch, dribbling on the floor at the thought of a big juicy bone.

Because anything shaped like food makes me want to chase after it!

'Me too!' yapped Oscar.

'All of us would, so why is she using an airship shaped like a bone?' Rocket wondered aloud, knowing that the evil empress usually preferred cat themes for her invasion attempts. 'There has to be a reason.'

'Maybe she's just stupid?' yapped Oscar.

'No,' said Butch.

Fluffkins is as mad as chocolate poop-scoop, but she's not stupid.

'The empress is crafty and cunning,' said Rocket, scratching his chin. 'And this big white bone has her mucky pawprints all over it.'

'I'm scanning the radio channels to pick up any audio signatures aboard the craft,' said Poppy, high-pitched warbling sounding through the ship as she moved though each bandwidth. 'But I can detect no feline frequencies.'

'No cats?' yapped Oscar, hoping for some fluffy foes to yap at.

'Then who else could it be?' asked Butch.

'Stop there!' said Rocket, tilting his head as he picked up a faint call amid the crackling static between two stations. 'Now lower the frequency and add a scramble-filter for canine communication.'

'Dogs?' Poppy frowned, but she followed the captain's order. He had the best hearing of all the Spacemutts and regularly picked up sounds that other dogs couldn't hear.

When the filter was added, all Spacemutts pricked up their ears as the transmission came through the speakers.

51

The signal was weak and distant, but it was definitely the sound of howling.

'OOOOOOOON

The Sausage Dog of Doom!

'A doggy distress call!' said Rocket, watching through the observation window as the giant airship hurtled towards Earth. 'And it's coming from inside that bone!'

'Are there alien dogs in space too?' yapped Oscar.

'With millions of planets in our galaxy there could well be dogs in hiding or on the run from the feline forces,' Rocket replied doubtfully. 'The only way we can know for sure is by making contact with the craft.'

The Spacemutts all gathered around

the cockpit as Poppy pulled on her headset and spoke into the microphone, transmitting on the same channel as the distress call.

> This is *Dogstar* calling unidentified craft. Come in, please,

she said, repeating the message several times but getting no reply. 'This is *Dogstar* answering your distress call. Please respond!'

The howling signal was growing weaker and weaker and then a sharp
yelp blasted through the speakers before the signal was lost for good. Butch and Poppy exchanged worried glances while  the mini dachshund filled the silence with yapping questions about what they planned to do. Rocket was the only dog with head still tilted and his ears pricked.

'WOOF,' he said eventually, 'did you make a backup recording of the doggy distress call?'

'Affirmative, Captain,' said the ship's computer.

'Play the last three seconds,' said Rocket, dashing to the central hub and opening a program that would convert the audio file into visual sound waves.

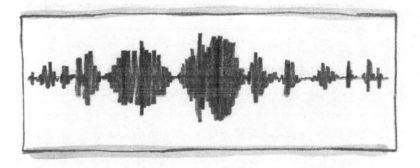

Poppy and Butch joined the captain at his station and watched.

As the high-pitched yelp sounded once again, Rocket moved his paws over the consol until the sound appeared as zigzag lines in a graph on the screen. Then he looped the audio while studying the image.

'There!' he said, eventually, paws moving over the touch screen to split the graph into two separate images. 'There was a digital code woven into the distress call!'

'What is it?' asked Poppy, as the symbols scrolled up the monitor.

'It's a hologram!' said Butch, recognizing the unique 3D code.

'Can you run it through the holoprojector?' Rocket asked WOOF.

'The code sequence is incomplete, Captain,' she replied as a wide beam of light appeared on the console. 'But I

should be able to pull something from the corrupted file.'

Suddenly a fuzzy 3D image of a chihuahua wearing a beret appeared in the light beam and the Spacemutts all jumped back. 'We are the Rebels United against Feline Foes . . . R.U.F.F. for short . . .' said the flickering blue hologram, its voice breaking up in the crackling static. '. . . some of us are wounded . . . we need your help, Spacemutts!'

The original message only ran for a few seconds and then played on a continuous loop until Rocket switched

off the holoprojector and turned to his crew.

'What do you think?' he asked.

'R.U.F.F.!' frowned Butch. 'Could there really be a band of rebel dogs?'

'I have a bad feeling,' said Poppy. 'It feels like a trap.'

'But what about the howling and the hologram?' yapped Oscar.

'Lady Fluffkins could have synthesized the howling,' said Butch.

'And the hologram was very grainy,' said Poppy.

'I agree with what you're saying,'

said Rocket, moving to the observation window and gazing out at the airship. 'But if there's even a slim chance there are dogs in distress aboard that curious craft, I can't stand by and do nothing.'

'Then we'll be right alongside you,' declared Poppy and Butch.

'Only one of us has to board the bone to investigate,' said Rocket, trotting to the back of the ship and pulling a spacesuit and helmet from the supply locker. 'I can do a space walkies and sneak aboard, while you two keep the *Dogstar* out of weapons range.'

gasped Poppy. 'It's much too dangerous.'

'I have to,' Rocket said firmly. 'You need to stay here to pilot the ship, and Butch is the only one who can work the engines to get everyone safely back home again.'

yapped Oscar.

The Sausage Dog of Doom!

'I have to sneak aboard without anyone knowing, just in case it is a trap,' smiled Rocket, patting the dachshund's head. 'And I think there's a very good chance they'll hear you coming.'

'I can be quiet!' yapped the sausage dog, and went on yapping about how quiet he could be if he really, really tried. 'As quiet as a mouse! A mouse wrapped in cotton wool! A mouse wrapped in cotton wool with a silencer on its tail!'

'Sorry, Oscar,' said Rocket, pulling on his helmet. 'I must go alone.'

'Not quite alone,' said Butch. 'You

can take *Rover* with you!'

'Who's Rover?' Rocket and Poppy asked together.

'It's not a who, it's a what!' said the bulldog, trotting away to pull the sheet from his latest invention and revealing a shiny metal shuttle. 'I've been working on it for months and this is the perfect time for a test drive.'

'WOW!' said Rocket, bounding over to the *Rover*. He leaped into the driving seat, gripped the control levers with his paws and peered eagerly through the visor. 'This is the coolest thing I've ever seen!'

'It's small enough not to be picked up on any feline radar, and the engine is whisper-quiet,' said Butch proudly. 'I built it for scouting missions in the Catnip Nebula so we could spy on Fluffkins without being detected.'

The bulldog showed the captain around the controls and then steered the *Rover* to the airlock in the cargo bay. Before closing the cockpit hatch, Rocket called out to Poppy.

'As my second in command, it's up to you to make sure that curious craft doesn't make it to Earth,' he said, looking

very serious. 'If I'm not back in one hour, you have to burst that airship and send it back to wherever it came from.'

'But . . .' Poppy protested.

'One hour, and that's an order,' said Rocket, pulling down the hatch.

Poppy nodded gravely as Butch sealed the cockpit and shot the shuttle out through the airlock. The pair then hurried over to the observation window and watched in silence as Rocket steered the *Rover* towards the giant inflated bone. The Spacemutts held their breath as the shuttle glided through open space

and then heaved a sigh of relief when it arrived unharmed and disappeared out of sight under the airship.

'Phew!' they whispered together, and then frowned.

'It's gone very quiet in here,' said Butch.

'Yes,' replied Poppy. 'Very quiet indeed.'

It took them a few more seconds to realize what this meant and then the two dogs slowly turned to face each other, eyes wide as they arrived at the same startling conclusion.

oScAr!

they gasped, bounding away to search the ship, hoping that the new recruit was hiding from them as a game, or had finally worn himself out and fallen asleep somewhere.

Poppy and Butch called out to the missing dachshund as they looked in the many little nooks where a mini dog could hide. But the usually yappy sausage dog was nowhere to be seen . . . or heard.

Shhh!

With the *Rover* securely docked on the underside of the giant airship, Rocket released the cockpit hatch and leaped aboard. The bone ship's structure was a complex skeleton of gas-filled chambers and stretched rubber that creaked and hissed creepily. The captain sniffed the air for any animal scent he could identify, but the smell of the gas in his nostrils overpowered his senses.

'Grrr,' he growled, and set off on foot.

The bone-white interior was a maze of damp, chilly corridors adding to the bleakness of the place. Rocket didn't want to stay any longer than he had to, so he raced through the ship at speed, paws bouncing on the spongy rubber floor.

Eventually he came upon a vast

circular door and skidded to a halt.

Peering through a round portal, Rocket could see a colossal white hall within. It had curved walls and a wide walkway leading to the distant cockpit, but there was no sign of any dogs. Then he looked closely at the pilot seat and saw a large brown tail wagging merrily.

Relieved to see a friendly waggy tail, the captain hit the paw-shaped release pad and the door split down the middle,

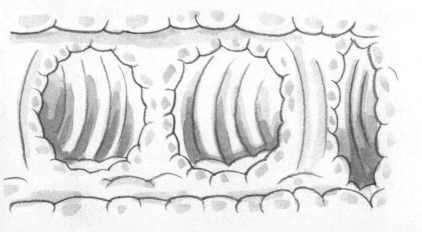

gliding open with a whisper-quiet whoosh
and closing again when he entered.

'Hello there!' called Rocket,
bounding through
the vast chamber of
curved walls that he
could now see were
filled with tiered
galleries of small white
archways. 'We picked up
a doggy distress call coming from this
ship. Are you in need of assistance?'

The tail continued to wag, but its
owner ignored him.

'Hello?' the captain repeated. 'Are you a member of . . .'

The white chair suddenly spun round, but instead of a friendly dog with a wagging tail to greet him, there was a hairless sphinx cat waving a long stick with brown fur stuck to it.

'R.U.F.F.?' barked Baldy, making the most of his role.

Realizing he'd walked into a trap, Rocket immediately turned tail and bounded back the way he'd come, but nearing the exit he saw the chihuahua from the hologram. It was grinning at him through the round portal in the door, and without the hazy 3D filter, he could see that something wasn't quite right.

The door glided open and a curious creature slunk into the chamber.

80

The Sausage Dog of Doom!

It had the head of a chihuahua wearing a green beret, but from the neck down it was a mass of snowy white fur! When the doors closed behind the abominable puffball, it ripped off the rubber mask with a sharp-clawed paw and pinged it across the room like a rubber band.

'Gotcha!' hissed Lady Fluffkins, combing out her flattened whiskers.

With his escape route temporarily blocked, Rocket skidded to a halt halfway down the catwalk and began circling with his head hung low, looking for an alternative exit.

'You don't really think you can hold me here?' he laughed.

'Not on my own, perhaps,' sniffed Fluffkins.

'Well, I don't think he'll be much use,' Rocket added, as Baldy quickly slithered past to join his mistress. The servant was still clutching the fake tail and was petting it lovingly.

'I wasn't talking about that fleshy fright!' growled the empress, snatching the furry stick from her hairless minion. 'Though Baldy does have some hidden talents.'

'Really?' said Rocket, stalling for time as he scanned the walls.

'Would you like to see him do an impersonation?' asked the Persian.

'An impersonation of who?' frowned Rocket.

In one swift movement Lady Fluffkins raised the furry stick and whacked the

servant's skinny tail, making him leap
high in the air while howling in pain.

OOOOOOWW WWWWW!

he howled.

'Sound familiar?' said the empress.

'The doggy distress call,' growled Rocket.

'Not enough to fool you on its own, of course,' explained Lady Fluffkins, licking her lips with evil glee. 'But dogs do love to dig, and I knew you would uncover the hidden hologram. And by then you'd be like a dog with a bone . . .'

'Mistress?' enquired Baldy, who was unfamiliar with the saying.

'Powerless to let it go!' hissed Fluffkins.

'Well, you can't keep me here, and the moment I get back to the *Dogstar* we'll

85

blast *this* bone to the other side of the galaxy, taking you and your mimicking minion with it,' Rocket delared.

'Oh, you're not going anywhere,' chuckled the empress, nodding to Baldy, who hurried away to press a button on the wall. 'I want you to have a ringside seat for the invasion of planet Earth.'

Rocket heard a faint humming and looked up in time to see that the galleries of archways were opening, each arched door slowly flipping up revealing small compartments with cats in them. The soundproof chambers had blocked out the rumbling purr from hundreds of Siamese cats.

'I love it when a cat-themed plan comes together,' said the empress.

'Cat theme?' Rocket frowned. 'We're in a giant dog bone!'

'A minor exterior detail to dumbfound you and your dopey dogs,' spat Fluffkins, puffing up her tail. 'On the inside we have copycats and cat flaps and catacombs and catwalks!'

The empress gave a silent signal and dozens of the cats immediately leaped down, wearing long white robes and matching headbands. They landed softly on the floor and in a few nimble leaps

and flips had formed a high wall around the dog.

'Woooooonnnngg . . .' the cats droned together in low Siamese voices, surrounding Rocket on all sides as a large open cage was lowered over him from the ceiling.

'The Siamese Samurai,' said Lady Fluffkins, waving the warriors back to their chambers as she stepped forward, slammed the cage door and locked it. 'They are the deadliest cats in the galaxy,' she added, tossing the key behind her for Baldy to catch.

'Well, they look weird,' laughed Rocket, stalling for time while he tried to come up with an escape plan. 'And they don't seem very deadly to me. In fact they all look half asleep!'

'They're meditating, you foolish fleabag,' growled the empress, slinking over to his cage.

> Siamese cats may be timid by nature, but they become lethal fighters when their minds are focused on their deadly martial arts.

'Which deadly martial arts, exactly?' asked Rocket.

'All of them,' grinned the empress.

'The Siamese Samurai begin their training as kittens on a silent mountain planet at the edge of the galaxy. These finely tuned killing machines are experts in judo, kung fu, ju-jitsu and kendo, to name but a few, all finely balanced with deep meditation. They are utterly unstoppable!'

Moments after the *Rover* had docked beneath the big bone balloon, Oscar had hopped from his hiding place in the cockpit and followed Rocket through the airship without making a sound.

The little dachshund didn't even yap when he saw the captain enter the main chamber and Lady Fluffkins' trap. He kept quiet and out of sight the whole time, knowing that he alone would have to rescue Rocket.

When the giant circular doors closed, Oscar had sniffed around outside the chamber and eventually found a tiny cat flap built into the rubber wall. He crept inside to find himself amid multi-storey catacombs filled with snoozing Siamese cats.

The sight of so many moggies made

the sausage dog want to yap more than anything else in his life, but he remained silent, stepping over their tails as he moved up through the kitty-cat catacombs, searching for an empty chamber. When he eventually found one, Oscar crept inside and peered down at the cage containing the leader of the Spacemutts. Lady Fluffkins and Baldy were busy at the cockpit, so the sausage dog waved a little paw, hoping to get the captain's attention.

Rocket was lying in the cage, furious that he'd been so easily tricked, but

relieved that the other Spacemutts were safe and would deal with the airship before the Siamese Samurai could reach planet Earth. He gazed up at the strange feline faces lining the walls of the massive central chamber, all deep in meditation. Then he saw one of them waving at him and almost gasped out loud when he realized it was Oscar.

Rocket quickly sat up and wagged his tail eagerly, while Oscar held a paw up to his mouth and uttered a sound that he had never made before.

'Shhh!' whispered the dachshund.

5

The Sausage Dog of Doom!

When he was trapped in the cage with no hope of escape, Rocket was willing to be shot across the galaxy along with the ship, so long as the other Spacemutts were safe and planet Earth was protected. But now he was watching Oscar swing silently down the wall like a gymnastic sausage, and his mind was racing with ideas about how to escape the cage and get the mini dachshund home.

His mind whirring, the captain leaped up and scanned the cockpit. Fluffkins and her servant were piloting the airship, which was obviously a two-cat job because Baldy was working doubly hard while the empress spat orders at him. Then Rocket looked around and spotted the key to his cage on a hook above them.

By the time Oscar had made it

down the wall, the captain had devised a plot to defeat the Siamese Samurai with the dachshund in the starring role. Tail wagging eagerly, the new recruit listened carefully to Rocket's instructions. Then, without saying a word, he nodded that he understood and quickly set to work on phase one: opening the cage!

Rocket could only watch as the sausage dog crept down the catwalk towards the front of the ship, freezing whenever one of the meditating moggies shifted or stirred around him, and when the brave little sausage dog reached the cockpit the captain held his breath.

The key to the cage was way out of reach for such a small dog, and if Oscar moved any closer the empress might see him, so he searched for something to lift the key and found the perfect thing: Baldy's fake dog's tail-on-a-stick.

Oscar crept around the empress and took the fluffy stick in his mouth. The brown fur tickled his nose and made him want to giggle and sneeze at the same time, but he focused on the task at hand and moved in on the prize. Tilting his head and craning his neck, the dachshund managed to unhook the key and quickly trotted away with it.

Rocket smiled proudly as Oscar returned with the key and swiftly released the lock,

while the captain held the cage door in his teeth so it wouldn't creak open, alerting the horde of cats around them.

'Are you ready to initiate phase two?' he whispered through the bars.

Oscar grinned and nodded with excitement.

Rocket released the cage door, which dropped down with a massive clang, and watched as hundreds of pairs of almond-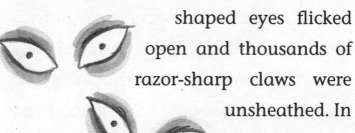shaped eyes flicked open and thousands of razor-sharp claws were unsheathed. In

the cockpit Lady
Fluffkins turned
towards the dogs,
raised her hackles
in anger and issued a simple order to her
deadly army.

'Get them!' she hissed.

The Siamese Samurai immediately
leaped from their chambers. Some
swung swords and jabbed daggers, while
others flicked nunchucks and warrior
staffs, but most of the cats we completely
unarmed, moving down the walls like
lightning, leaping and rolling and

landing in lethal kung-fu poses.

The cats had the dogs surrounded in no time so Rocket jumped up on to the cage, using the furry stick to fend off any

overhead attacks. Oscar couldn't jump so high, so he remained at ground level, looking helpless as the advancing army closed in.

'What a cowardly captain you are!' mocked Lady Fluffkins, slinking though the ranks of Siamese Samurai. 'You leave your helpless mini fleabag to fend for himself, while you take the only weapon.'

'Oscar may look helpless, but he has hidden talents,' said Rocket, tearing two lumps of faux fur from the stick.

He is the mighty Sausage Dog of Doom and he has the power to defeat your entire army single-handed.

'No one can defeat the Siamese Samurai! And certainly not a dinky little dog that can't even grow proper legs!' scoffed the empress, laughing at the dachshund. 'Their minds are completely in tune through deep meditation . . .'

'Oh, yes, the meditation,' Rocket interrupted, stuffing the tufts of fur in his ears. 'I expect they need lots of peace and quiet so they can focus on all of those martial arts and deadly skills you mentioned?'

Before Fluffkins could answer, Rocket nodded to Oscar and then watched with

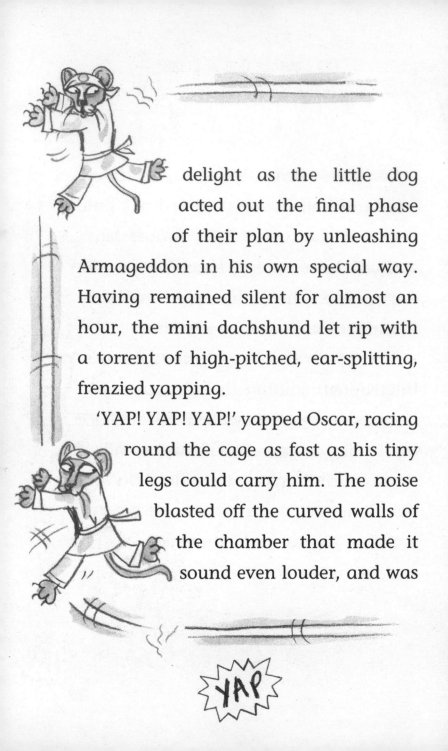

delight as the little dog acted out the final phase of their plan by unleashing Armageddon in his own special way. Having remained silent for almost an hour, the mini dachshund let rip with a torrent of high-pitched, ear-splitting, frenzied yapping.

'YAP! YAP! YAP!' yapped Oscar, racing round the cage as fast as his tiny legs could carry him. The noise blasted off the curved walls of the chamber that made it sound even louder, and was

YAP

YAP

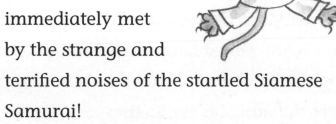

immediately met
by the strange and
terrified noises of the startled Siamese
Samurai!

'WOWOWOWOWOOOONG!'
they squealed.

The cats leaped away to escape
the deafening Dog of Doom,
clinging to the walls with their
razor-sharp claws and yowling with
fright. A life of silent meditation had
definitely not prepared them for the
yappiest yapper in the universe.

YAP

'Get your claws out of my airship, you fools!' yelled Lady Fluffkins, but the frightened felines could hear nothing over the wall of noise, so they didn't even notice when tiny hissing holes appeared in the rubber.

'TIME TO GO, OSCAR!' barked Rocket, but not even his booming voice could be heard above the yapping and yowling and increasingly loud hissing of air, so he leaped down from the cage, grabbed the dachshund by the collar and bounded towards the exit.

With Oscar still yapping, Rocket hit the

door release with a paw and bolted down the maze of hallways, walls sagging and shrivelling around them, while Lady Fluffkins tried to command hundreds of hysterical cats to retract their claws.

But it was already too late.

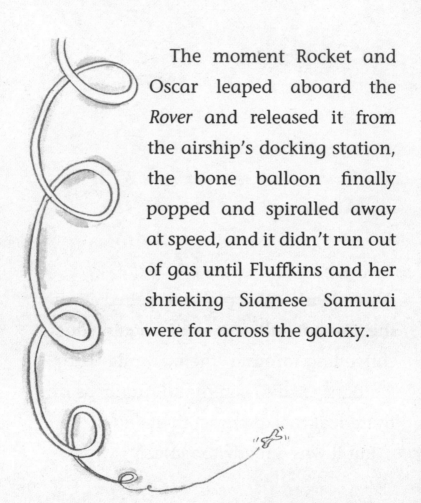

The moment Rocket and Oscar leaped aboard the *Rover* and released it from the airship's docking station, the bone balloon finally popped and spiralled away at speed, and it didn't run out of gas until Fluffkins and her shrieking Siamese Samurai were far across the galaxy.

Silent Sausage Dog

'Do you think we've dealt with Lady Fluffkins once and for all?' asked Oscar, as the Spacemutts returned to the Pooch Pound just in time for morning visitors. 'Because then we can all behave ourselves and find new homes.'

'I don't think so, little one,' said Rocket. 'The feline forces are all over the galaxy. Someone will have picked up the empress and returned her to the Catnip Nebula, where she will no doubt be plotting another invasion.'

'But Earth is safe for now, thanks to you,' said Butch.

'How did you do it, Oscar?' asked Poppy, having wondered about this all the way home. 'How did you manage to stay quiet for so long, especially with so many cats around?'

'I remembered something the captain told me,' said the dachshund.

'What *did* I say?' Rocket frowned.

'*Sometimes it's smart to be silent,*' whispered Oscar. 'And it worked so well that I'm going to try it out on the visitors today.'

'Then I don't think you'll be here long,' laughed Rocket. 'And when you go to your new home, you can help the Spacemutts by saving up your yaps for any cats that you see acting suspiciously.'

'Yes, Captain,' said the sausage dog. He tried to do a paw salute but his tiny legs couldn't quite reach, so he wagged his tail instead.

Proud to be of service to the Spacemutts.

Oscar kept wagging his tail all day long when the visitors arrived. He was excited by all of the happy people making a fuss over him, but managed to stay calm and greet them nicely, while Rocket, Butch and Poppy were making a racket in their kennels.

By the end of the day the mini dachshund had caught the attention of one particular family with lots of noisy

children who would never leave him
alone for long or mind the odd yapping
fit. Because even though it's sometimes

smart to be silent, it's also lovely to be loud from time to time.

When it was time for Oscar to go to his new home, the family led him past the other three kennels and chuckled with joy when Oscar gave each of his kennel mates a happy yappy goodbye.

As the warden closed the doors for the night, Rocket, Butch and Poppy settled on their blankets to sleep in peace and quiet. They were all tired, but very proud of how the deafening dachshund had managed to become a silent sausage dog to save planet Earth.

The Spacemutts dreamed of capturing Lady Fluffkins soon, so that they could start behaving for the visitors and find loving families who would offer them a happy home too.

Maybe next time . . .

SPACE MUTTS

FLUFFY ASSASSINS FROM MARS!

MICHAEL BROAD

Earth: The final frontier in the epic battle between cats and dogs

The evil empress Lady Fluffkins has launched a fleet of deadly flying saucers from Mars, and it's up to the plucky Spacemutts to save the world (again!). But their newest recruit, Scamp, is only a puppy. Is he ready to be a hero?

MICHAEL BROAD

Earth: The final frontier in the epic battle between cats and dogs

Meet the poshest poodle in the universe! New recruit Monty won't ever get his paws dirty, even on an intergalactic mission. But when a huge horrible hairball is hurtling towards Earth, will Monty learn to muck in when his friends need him most?